Sailor Anna Goes to Sea

Reach for the stars, be inspired and continue to dream!
Brianna Snider

Copyright © 2018 Brianna Snider

All rights reserved.

ISBN: 1986739910
ISBN-13: 978-1986739917

DEDICATION

This book is dedicated to my husband Blaine and our two children Sienna and Kohan.

Look for Salty the crab on every page!

Hi! My name is Anna. My friends call me Sailor Anna because I just love the ocean.

This is my little brother, Kash, and his dog Max. "Woof, woof"! We all love the ocean and we are about to head on a big adventure to explore and learn about different marine life.

We've borrowed our dad's ship called the Singing Mermaid. We made sure we asked first.

Keep a sharp lookout for Captain Catfish. He's a mean old pirate with a long grey beard, and will try to steal our ship if we're not careful. He always sings a merry sailing tune so we can hear him coming.

Every good sailor keeps a sharp lookout and listens carefully at all times when sailing the seven seas.

Before we leave, we need to prepare. I've asked Kash to check the weather forecast to make sure there are no storms up ahead.

Next, we need to make sure we have enough food for our trip and stock the ship's galley. We can't forget Max's dog treats!

I've also made sure we have our nautical charts and safety equipment onboard, and we can't forget our most important piece of equipment. Do you know what that is?

Our life jackets. That's right! Every good sailor wears a life jacket to stay safe on the water in case you fall in.

Let's set sail. Say "let go the lines" and Kash will let them go. We're on our way!

Look to the compass to see which way we are heading. North, East, South, or West. The arrow is pointing up to the letter N. North, that's right! We will head north.

To find our way north, we can use the navigation star called the North Star. It is the biggest star and shines the brightest in the night sky.

Now, we are on our way to the Arctic Ocean. There, we will be searching for Beluga whales to take pictures of in the wild. Look for other marine life along the way.

My brother, Kash, and his dog Max will be on the lookout for icebergs. We don't want to run into one.

Did you know that an iceberg is much, much bigger under the water than it is on the surface?

Can you see an iceberg up ahead? Right, there is one directly in front of us and we are heading straight for it! Should we turn port (left) or starboard (right) to avoid hitting it?

Starboard, that's right! Let's turn the ship's wheel until we are safe from danger. Say "turn, turn, turn". Great job, we avoided the iceberg!

"Woof, woof". What is it Max? Did you spot something? Look, just off of the port beam. There is a baby polar bear on the iceberg looking for its mom.

Do you see the baby polar bear's mom? There she is, she's searching for food so the baby polar bear can eat its dinner. Let's help the baby polar bear find its mom. Yell to the baby polar bear and say "jump". "Jump, jump, jump".

Yay, you did it. The baby polar bear jumped and found its mom.

Let's continue on our adventure in search for Beluga whales. Beluga whales tend to stay in pods near the Arctic shoreline. They are some of the smallest whales on earth.

Let's keep a sharp lookout for a pod of white Beluga whales and their grey babies.

Oh no, I hear someone singing a merry sailing tune! It's Captain Catfish and he's heading this way! We can't let him come onboard our ship. If he does, he will take the Singing Mermaid!

Say "Walk the plank Captain Catfish". He's walking the plank back onboard his ship. That was close. He almost took the Singing Mermaid. Great work everyone.

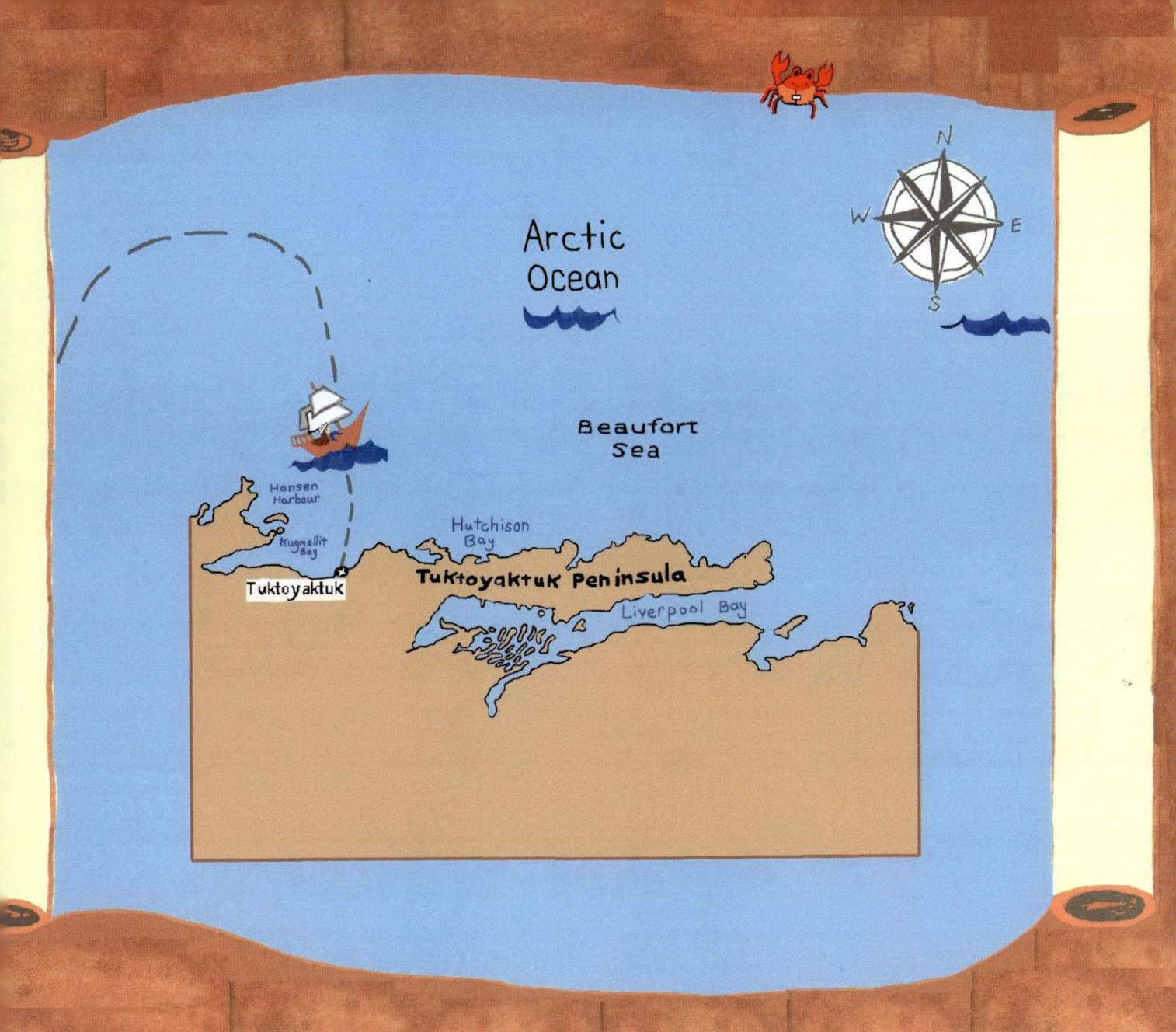

We are now heading towards the Arctic port called Tuktoyaktuk. (Tuck-toy-yuck-tuck) "Tuk" for short, and is located in the Northwest Territories in Canada.

Kash just heard on the VHF radio that there were a pod of Beluga whales spotted just north of Tuk. Let's check it out!

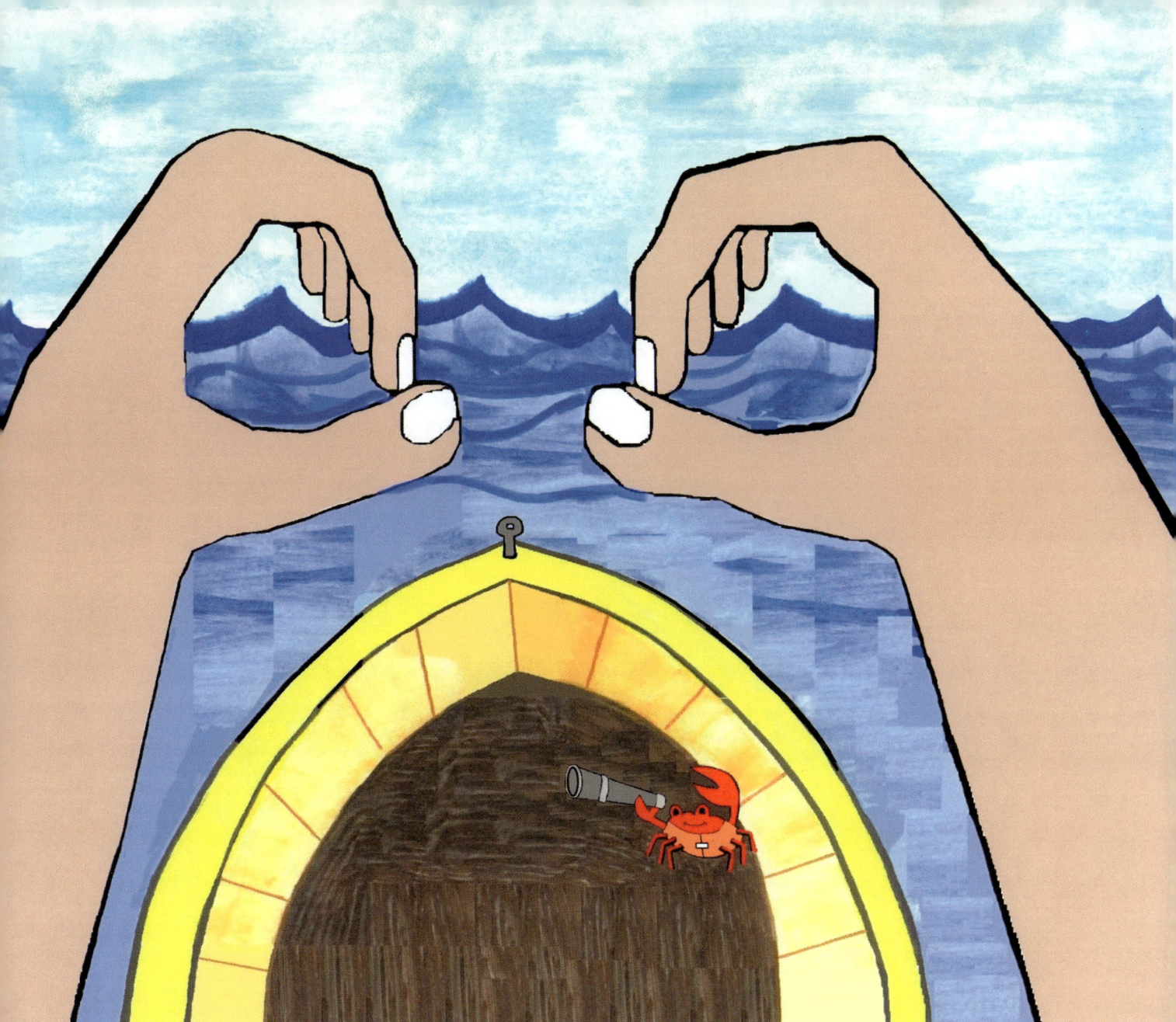

Let's make binoculars with our fingers and see if we can spot the Beluga whales. Can you spot the Beluga pod?

Look for shiny white heads bobbing in and out of the water. There they are, we found them! Excellent work.

Let's take a picture and watch them play.

One of the baby Beluga's is playing peek-a-boo with Max.
Say "peek-a-boo!"

Oh no, the baby Beluga whale spat water at Max! Poor Max. Now he's all wet!

What a great way to end our journey to the Arctic Ocean. Thank you for joining us. See you next time!

Nautical terms in the book

Ahead- In front of

Anchor- A heavy metal hook thrown overboard to keep a ship in place.

Anchorage- A safe place to anchor the ship

Beam- Beside the ship to the port or starboard

Binoculars- A tool used to see far away

Captain- The person in charge on a ship

Compass- A tool used to find north, south, east and west

Galley- A kitchen on a ship or boat

Let go of the lines- To untie the lines holding the ship to the dock

Life jackets- Are safety jackets that float

Lookout- A person who keeps a sharp lookout around for obstacles and dangers

Nautical Charts- Maps of the ocean and land

Navigational Star- A star in the sky used to help navigate a ship at sea on a clear night

Onboard- On the ship

Pirate- A person who steals treasure and ships

Port- To the left of the ship when looking ahead

Ports- A place/dock where ships can seek refuge

Sail the seven seas- To sail in all seven seas around the world

Sail/Sailing- When the ship is moving

Sailor- A person who sails

Set Sail- To leave the dock or anchorage and head to sea

Ship- A big boat

Wheel- A wheel you turn to steer the ship

Starboard- To the right of the ship when looking ahead

Steer- To steer the ships wheel

VHF radio- Very High Frequency radio

Made in the USA
Columbia, SC
10 May 2018